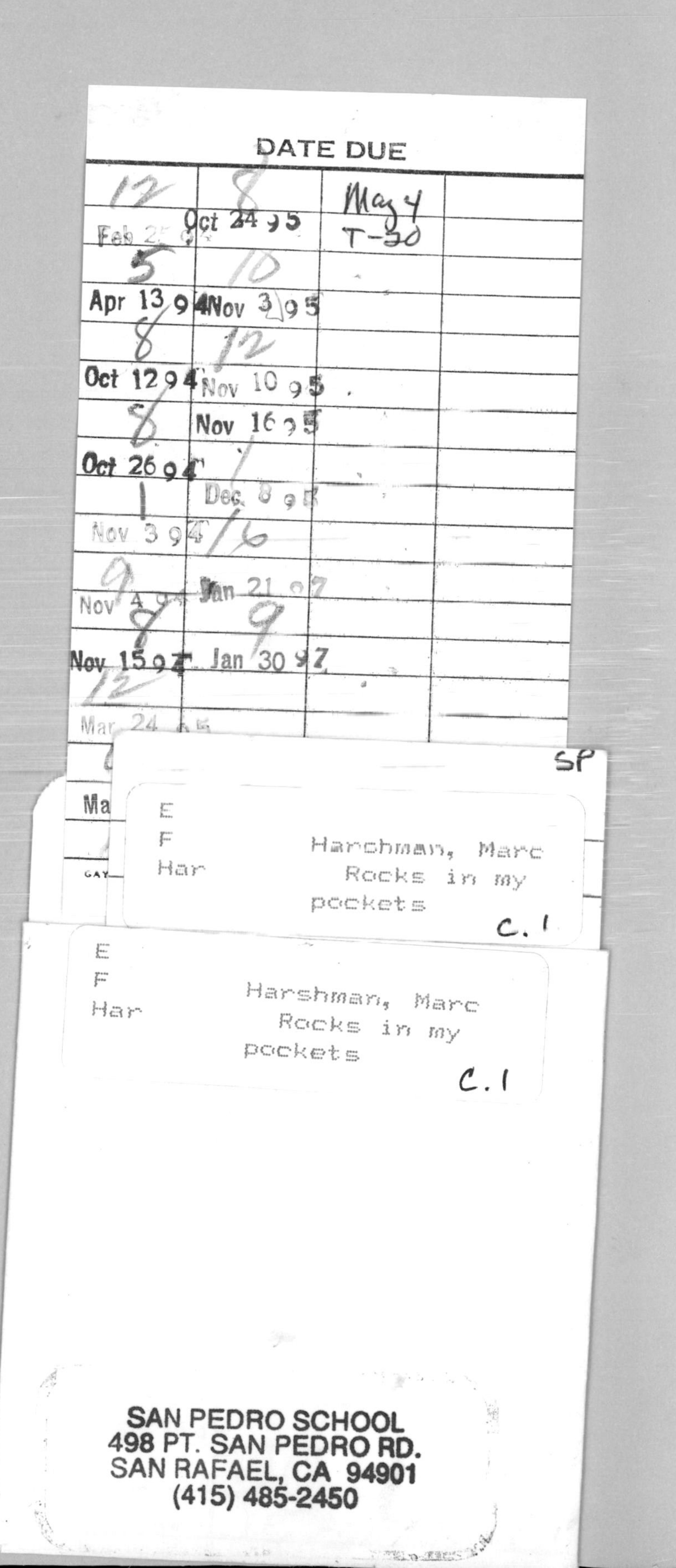
DATE DUE
E
F
Har
Harshman, Marc
Rocks in my
pockets
C. 1
SAN PEDRO SCHOOL
498 PT. SAN PEDRO RD.
SAN RAFAEL, CA 94901
(415) 485-2450

ROCKS IN MY POCKETS

ROCKS IN MY POCKETS

MARC HARSHMAN
and BONNIE COLLINS

Illustrated by TONI GOFFE

COBBLEHILL BOOKS/DUTTON · NEW YORK

Library of Congress Cataloging-in-Publication Data
Harshman, Marc.
Rocks in my pockets / Marc Harshman ; illustrated by Toni Goffe.
p. cm.
Summary: The rocks around their mountain farm serve all of the
Woods family in many ways, both utilitarian and recreational,
until the day two ladies from the city come to visit.
ISBN 0-525-65055-5
[1. Rocks—Fiction. 2. Mountain life—Fiction.]
I. Goffe, Toni, ill. II. Title.
PZ7.H256247 Ro 1991
[E]—dc20 90-32122
CIP
AC

Published in the United States by
Cobblehill Books, an affiliate of Dutton Children's Books,
a division of Penguin Books USA Inc.

Typography by Kathleen Westray
Printed in Hong Kong First Edition
10 9 8 7 6 5 4 3 2 1

For Bonnie
—MH

For my children—
Linda, Barbara, Sandra, and Thomas
—BC

To Kirstin—keep on drawing
—TG

To start at the beginning, the Woods family lived on a farm on top of the top of the highest mountain in these parts, a way up where the wind is your neighbor all year round. The farm was on old rocky soil, but it was the best the family could afford and so they worked out a living any way they could.

They'd raise knee-high corn

and walnut-sized potatoes and call them a good crop. You'd hear no complaints.

Their house was drafty, their animals skinny, and their clothes patched out of what was at hand. But one thing they all did have was pockets, and that was mighty important, for in the pockets they carried the rocks. Rocks? Yes, rocks.

Every morning when they'd set out to work—Father and Mother, Grandpa, and Tommy and Jenny—Father would always say, "Be sure ye put some rocks in your pockets now. Put them rocks in your pockets or the wind will be likely to blow ye away." And he was right, for the wind did blow fierce across their mountaintop fields.

So Father and Mother and Grandpa and Tommy and Jenny would all pick up rocks and carry them in their pockets off into the fields. And not a one of them was ever blown away.

The rocks were a lot of fun, too. Tommy and Jenny would often play pass with them or hide-and-find games.

And even Mother and Father and Grandpa would frequently worry the stones around in their pockets—"Just good to know they're there," Grandpa would say. "Who knows where my old dry bones would end up if this wind ever got a hold of me?"

In the evening after supper, Grandpa or Mother or Father would often tell a story they remembered from the early days. As the tales were told you might see one or the other of them rubbing one of the rocks in their hands.

In the cold of winter, these same rocks would be set in the fire and then taken out and wrapped in heavy socks to lay between the cold covers. They were, as any of the family could have told you, mighty handy rocks.

There was always a heap of them, smooth and slick, strewn by the chimney, gleaming from all the rubbing and polishing they got. But once, after a hard winter and a miserable spring, the rocks became more than handy. They became…well, you'll see.

One day in early summer a couple of high fancy ladies from the city came by looking for antiques, for what might impress their neighbors.

But the Woodses didn't have much in the way of antiques. Nope, Father Woods said, they didn't have anything to sell. But just then one of the ladies noticed the pile of rocks by the chimney.

"My, but aren't those beautiful!" exclaimed the one.

"Indeed," echoed the other. And they were kind of pretty, slick as glass, bright as the stars, with colors in them that just showed right through.

"Well, well, we've never seen stones like this before. What kind are they?" asked the first.

"Well, I don't really know them by any name. They're just plain old rocks."

"Would you sell them to us?"

"Well, I don't really have any reason to sell them to you."

"Oh, but we'd pay you a fair price. They're kind of rare, now, aren't they?"

Well, Father Woods began to catch on then, and he said, "Well, yes, maybe they are. You don't see many of this kind where you come from, I guess."

"What would you take for them?" the ladies asked sweetly.

And then he told them a reasonable price and they paid him. And, were those ladies thrilled! From the way they talked there wouldn't be anybody in all of Pittsburgh, or New York, or wherever they came from, that had stones like these.

So, they went back to their homes, put their stones on display, and bragged all over them.

That night after supper, Father said, "Well, the corn's big enough to hoe in the morning, but before you kids go out, find a bunch of new rocks and get 'em into your pockets. Bring some back for your Mom and Grandpa, and then we'll all grab us some more later. Who knows, we might be in the rock-selling business."

And that was true enough. Folks started coming from cities and towns, near and far.

The money the Woods family made from those rocks drove the hard times from their door for good. Now, they didn't give up farming or their mountaintop, but it was easier with a little extra money to have more feed for the animals, warmer clothes, and so on.

But, of course, there were people who tried to take advantage. They would come out from the cities and ask around about those stones.

They'd tell Father Woods that those by the chimney weren't quite right and ask him if he knew where they might find some similar ones. Father Woods, being an honest man, would tell them.

And those folks, eyes as big as slab-sided sandstones, would go gather up a heap of field rocks. They thought they were awfully clever not having to pay Father Woods that way.

But, of course, those rocks never quite shone the way the ones in the chimney corner did and nobody back in the city was ever impressed by them, either. And those folks that took them will never figure out why.

I guess they never lived on top of the top of the highest mountain; never carried those rocks in their pockets all day long—hoeing, stooping—spring, summer, fall, and winter; never played pass with them; never curled under a blanket with those rocks nestled between their feet;

never sat around a fireplace rubbing those rocks while the old stories about hard work and patience filled their heads. No, I bet they never did.

But I have, and these rocks in my pockets still keep my feet on the ground in even the windiest weather.